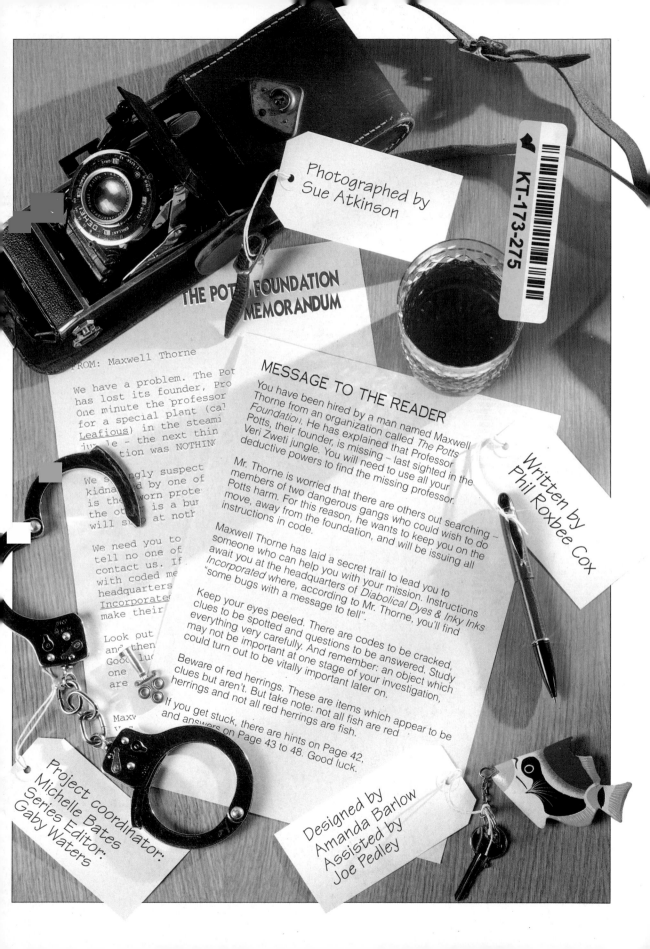

Photographed by
Sue Atkinson

Written by
Phil Roxbee Cox

THE POTTS FOUNDATION MEMORANDUM

FROM: Maxwell Thorne

We have a problem. The Pot[ts]
has lost its founder, Pro[fessor]
One minute the professor
for a special plant (cal[led]
Leafious) in the steami[ng]
jun[g]le – the next thin[g]
[posi]tion was NOTHIN[G]

We s[tro]ngly suspect
kidna[pp]ed by one of
is the [s]worn prote
the oth[er] is a bu[r]
will st[op] at noth[ing]

We need you to
tell no one of
contact us. If
with coded me
headquarters
Incorporated
make their

Look out
and then
Good luc[k]
one
are

Max[well]

MESSAGE TO THE READER

You have been hired by a man named Maxwell Thorne from an organization called *The Potts Foundation*). He has explained that Professor Veri Zweti Potts, their founder, is missing – last sighted in the Veri Zweti jungle. You will need to use all your deductive powers to find the missing professor.

Mr. Thorne is worried that there are others out searching – members of two dangerous gangs who could wish to do Potts harm. For this reason, he wants to keep you on the move, away from the foundation, and will be issuing all instructions in code.

Maxwell Thorne has laid a secret trail to lead you to someone who can help you with your mission. Instructions await you at the headquarters of *Diabolical Dyes & Inky Inks Incorporated* where, according to Mr. Thorne, you'll find "some bugs with a message to tell"

Keep your eyes peeled. There are codes to be cracked, clues to be spotted and questions to be answered. Study everything very carefully. And remember: an object which may not be important at one stage of your investigation, could turn out to be vitally important later on.

Beware of red herrings. These are items which appear to be clues but aren't. But take note: not all fish are red herrings and not all red herrings are fish.

If you get stuck, there are hints on Page 42, and answers on Page 43 to 48. Good luck.

Project coordinator:
Michelle Bates
Series Editor:
Gaby Waters

Designed by
Amanda Barlow
Assisted by
Joe Pedley

2

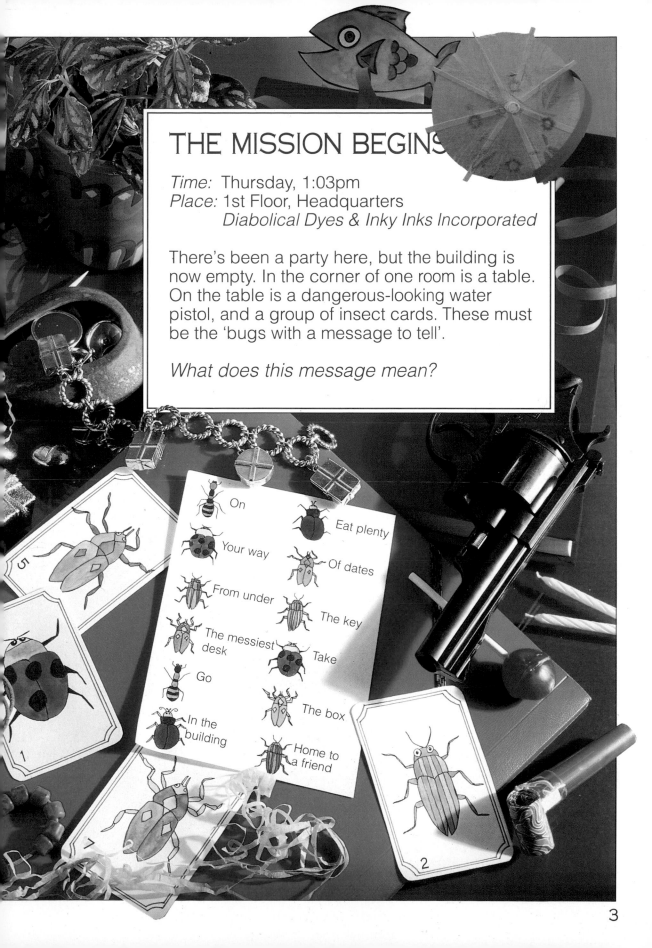

THE MISSION BEGINS

Time: Thursday, 1:03pm
Place: 1st Floor, Headquarters
  Diabolical Dyes & Inky Inks Incorporated

There's been a party here, but the building is now empty. In the corner of one room is a table. On the table is a dangerous-looking water pistol, and a group of insect cards. These must be the 'bugs with a message to tell'.

What does this message mean?

On

Eat plenty

Your way

Of dates

From under

The key

The messiest desk

Take

Go

The box

In the building

Home to a friend

THE SEARCH IS ON

Time: Thursday, 1:37pm
Place: The messiest desk, 120th Floor, Headquarters
   Diabolical Dyes & Inky Inks Incorporated

The message mentioned a key under a box of dates.
There's certainly plenty of other fruit around, but not one of
them is a date or even a fig, which is the next best thing.
There are boxes too – a flowery one, and one shaped like
an Egyptian sarcophagus. Both are empty. There's nothing
in them, on them, or under them. The clock has stopped,
but there's no key under it either. A waste of time?

Where is the key hidden?

DEEP IN THE VAULT

Time: Thursday, 2:18pm
Place: Third National Bank, Uptown

Box 33
3rd National
Bank
Thrift Street

GP 2285 7
141

The key opens a safety deposit box at the address shown on the tag. Inside the box is a bundle of money in an envelope marked **EXPENSES**, a few oddments, some coded instructions, and a gallery of torn up photographs.

*PhReOrFeEiSsSaOcRaPrOkTeTySbPeRlOoFnEgSiSnOgRtPoOt
ThTeSoPnReOpFeErSsSoOnRpPhOoTtToSgPrRaOpFhEeSdSw
OiRtPhOoTuTtSaPnRaOnFiEmSaSlOvRiPsOiTtTtShPeRpOeFr
EsSoSnOaRtPoOnTcTeS*

What do these instructions say?

7

DEAD END!

Time: Thursday, 3:27pm
Place: Dr. Karl Otta's *Plant Import Export Company*, Downtown

On the back of the bearded man's photo is the name Dr. Karl Otta and an address: Plant Import Export Company, 12a Flash St., Downtown. This is a grand title for a stuffy little office above a sock factory. The room is buzzing with bugs but Dr. Karl Otta doesn't seem to mind. He's very dead. Probably murdered.

If he was murdered, how recently could it have happened?

THE SEARCH FOR CLUES

Time: Thursday, 3:57pm
Place Dr. Karl Otta's car. Parking Lot.
Rear of *Plant Import Export Company*

The car key from the safety deposit box unlocks Karl Otta's old car. There is a pile of odds and ends on the passenger seat. A golf ball . . . a bottle of poison . . . a starting pistol . . . a crystal ball . . . There's something familiar here. A symbol? A sign?

What is it?

THE SNAKE BITE CLUB

It's party time again!

Why not slither your way down to AL'S for a night to remember.

Everyone welcome Friday September 8th

Not only snakes have scales. Pianos do too. Learn to play the easy way. Ask at the bar for details.

Plan to travel far? Then why not rent a car? TOOTS CAR RENTAL has car for you. Near or far, rent a TOOTS CAR.
Phone: 555-000-555-000

ALL HATS AND COATS TO BE CHECKED IN ON ARRIVAL. DON'T LOSE YOUR TICKET.
NO TICKET, NO COAT.

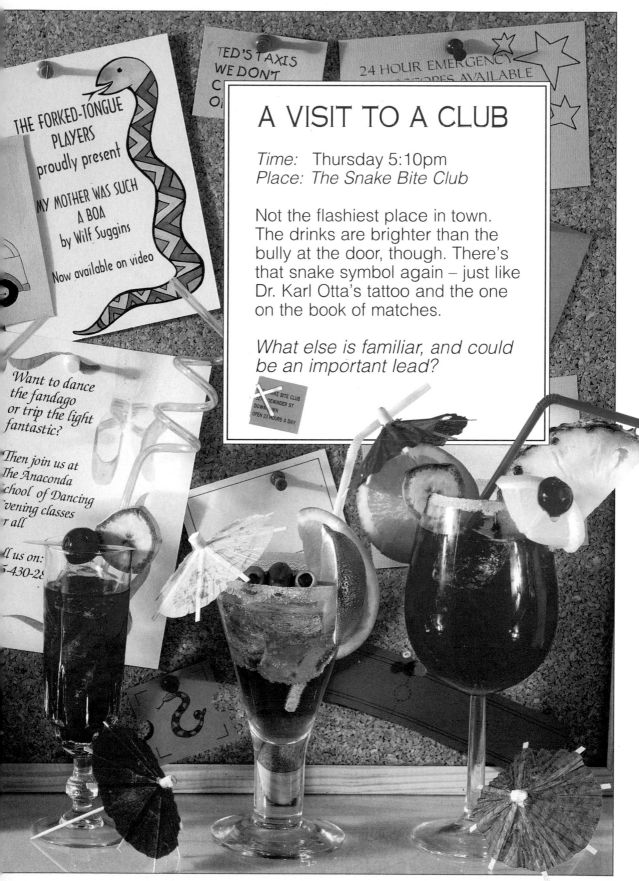

THE FORKED-TONGUE PLAYERS
proudly present
MY MOTHER WAS SUCH A BOA
by Wilf Suggins

Now available on video

TED'S TAXIS
WE DON'T
C...
O...

24 HOUR EMERGENCY
...ORES AVAILABLE

Want to dance the fandago or trip the light fantastic?

Then join us at The Anaconda School of Dancing Evening classes for all

Call us on:
5-430-28...

A VISIT TO A CLUB

Time: Thursday 5:10pm
Place: The Snake Bite Club

Not the flashiest place in town. The drinks are brighter than the bully at the door, though. There's that snake symbol again – just like Dr. Karl Otta's tattoo and the one on the book of matches.

What else is familiar, and could be an important lead?

SNAKE BITE CLUB
SIDEWINDER ST
DOWN TOWN
OPEN 23 HOURS A DAY

DEAD MAN'S CLOTHES

Time: Thursday, 5:33pm
Place: A doorway. Across the street from
the *Snake Bite Club*

In return for the pink ticket from the safety deposit
box, comes a coat with the name *K. OTTA* sewn
onto the lining, with a message: *IF FOUND, PLEASE
RETURN TO OWNER'S OFFICE*. The coat was heavy.
No wonder. There was masses of stuff in the
pockets. The contents now lie in a doorway, lighted
by a street lamp. Most of it looks like garbage.
Most of it *is* garbage, and the money is bad news.

141

Why?

RANSACKED!

Time: Thursday, 5:45pm
Place: Dr. Karl Otta's *Plant Import
and Export Company*
Returning coat to (dead) owner

Someone else has paid Dr. Karl Otta's office
a visit. It could be the cleaners because the
body has certainly been cleared away . . .
but that's unlikely. The rest of the place is
such a mess and the bugs haven't been
dusted. The visitor has taken more than just
the body, and dropped something too.

*What is missing, and
what's new?*

This is Potts's journal, a map of Sprunga Leeki, and a model of a village.

My secret sign

A friendly bug

My whereabouts:
Some Quiz Us About
Recent Expedition And
They Have Reservations,
Expecting Excitement!

PLANS MAPPED OUT

Time: Friday, 9:11am
Place: Fairly Central Park,
        after a restless night

A large package has arrived. Inside is a book that was on the table at *Diabolical Dyes & Inky Inks Incorporated*. It's Professor Potts's journal. There's also a model village and a map. And a coded clue to the professor's last-known location.

Where, on the map, was Potts?

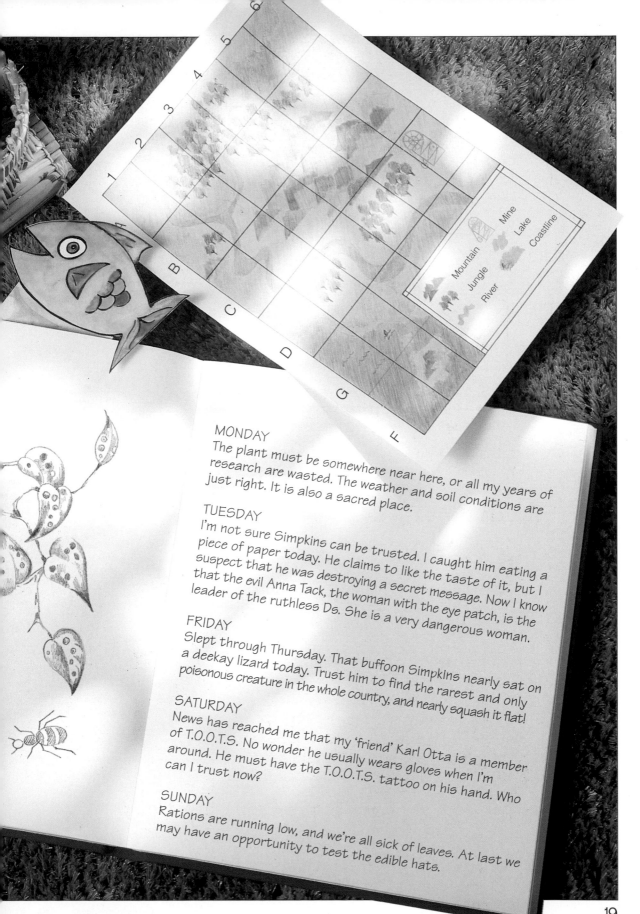

Mountain Mine
Jungle Lake
River Coastline

MONDAY
The plant must be somewhere near here, or all my years of research are wasted. The weather and soil conditions are just right. It is also a sacred place.

TUESDAY
I'm not sure Simpkins can be trusted. I caught him eating a piece of paper today. He claims to like the taste of it, but I suspect that he was destroying a secret message. Now I know that the evil Anna Tack, the woman with the eye patch, is the leader of the ruthless Ds. She is a very dangerous woman.

FRIDAY
Slept through Thursday. That buffoon Simpkins nearly sat on a deekay lizard today. Trust him to find the rarest and only poisonous creature in the whole country, and nearly squash it flat!

SATURDAY
News has reached me that my 'friend' Karl Otta is a member of T.O.O.T.S. No wonder he usually wears gloves when I'm around. He must have the T.O.O.T.S. tattoo on his hand. Who can I trust now?

SUNDAY
Rations are running low, and we're all sick of leaves. At last we may have an opportunity to test the edible hats.

19

UP IN THE AIR

Time: Friday, 12:35pm
Place: Seat D5. *Flight 01424* to
Sprunga Leeki on the way
to finding Potts's last
known location

The person in seat D6 is laying
cards onto a briefcase on her lap.
She's the woman with the feather
boa in one of the photographs from
the safety deposit box. What's her
game? Not just cards, that's for sure.
An item on her briefcase suggests it
is something far deadlier . . .

What is it?

DOWN TO EARTH

Time: Friday 3:06pm local time
Place: Runway,
        Sprunga Leeki Airport

It's hot. The temperature is somewhere between sweltering and unbearable. A fellow passenger drops his case on the runway. Things tumble and roll everywhere. From the look of his dice, he's not the sort of person to leave anything to chance. He also seems to have something fishy in more ways than one.

What is it?

TREASURE CHEST?

Time: Friday, 3:19pm local time
Place: Hangar H, Sprunga Leeki Airport

The biplane chartered to fly to the Veri Zweti jungle is inside this shack they call a hangar. In the corner is an open trunk spilling over with oddments. The skin of a recently eaten banana lies on the ground – but this is no time for slip ups. That spotted creature has been spotted somewhere before . . .

But where?

TO THE JUNGLE!

Time: Friday, 5:12pm local time
Place: Veri Zweti jungle, at location
recorded in Potts's journal

The biplane has landed in a
clearing. Through the trees is a rock
just waiting to be found and,
beyond that, an ancient, ruined
temple covered in creepy creepers.
This must be the 'sacred place' that
the professor wrote about in the
journal. Potts has left behind a very
simple message.

What is it?

HOT ON THE TRAIL

Time: Friday, 5:47pm local time
Place: Veri Zweti jungle, in the
ruined temple at the end of
the arrow trail

Professor Potts's trail of arrows
ends by a wall, and with a
message in a water bottle. At first
glance, the message makes
about as much sense as eating
soup with a fork.

What does it say?

My life is in great danger now that I have found the special plant. It only grows inside the ruins of this great temple and is of interest to two powerful organizations. One, The Order Of The Serpent, has kept this location a secret for a thousand years. Each member has a special snake tattoo.

The other organization has evil aims. Called the Dominants, its members plan to use some of the special plant's powers as a mind control drug. They want to turn the population into mindless slaves. They each wear the ring of the Evil Eye.

Both groups want to stop my work. I'll only be safe when the report on my discoveries here is published. It includes the formula to an antidote to the mind control drug. Once that is done, it will be too late for them to try to silence me. Until then, I shall go into hiding. So, whoever is reading this, please understand that I don't want to be found. Go home.

SNAKE TROUBLE!

Time: Friday, 7:23 local time
Place: Lost somewhere in the
Veri Zweti jungle, searching
for the biplane

Nightfall. There's a light up ahead, but
it's not coming from the biplane.
There's a candle and a fruit feast for
snake lovers. Toy snakes are
everywhere . . . and, in among them,
one that's very much alive and
slithering from a box of half-eaten hats.

Is the snake dangerous?

A STRANGE DISCOVERY

Time: Friday, 8:24pm local time
Place: Inside a brightly-lit house
in a jungle clearing

Still lost. Outside it's dark and raining hard.
Inside, there's no one around. The front door
was open . . . but is this house really an ideal
place to shelter from a storm? Everywhere
seems warm and inviting. There's even a bed
to sleep on if these things are cleared off it.
But something feels wrong.

*Is this really a safe place to spend
the night?*

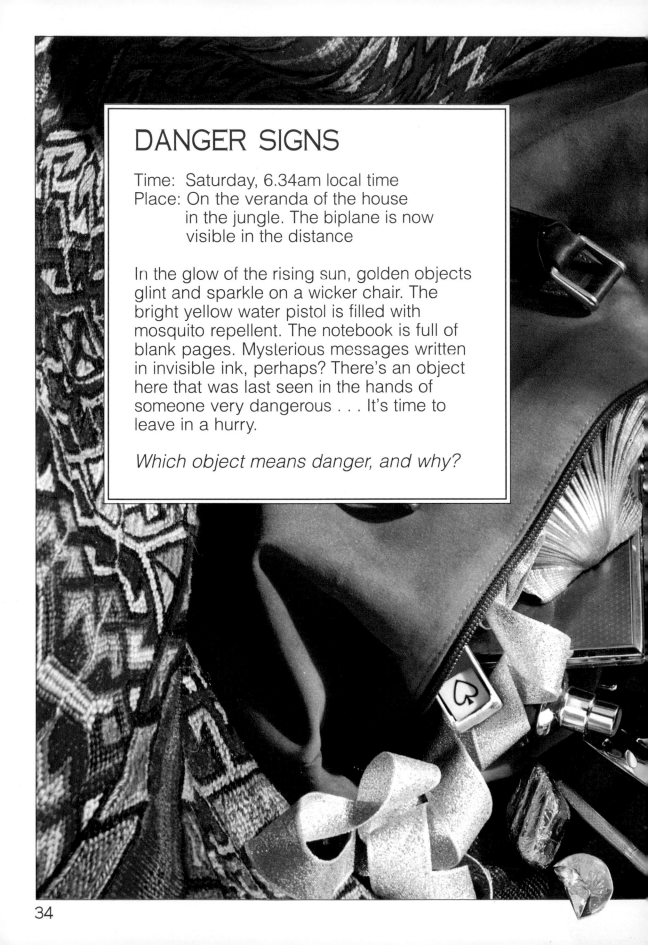

DANGER SIGNS

Time: Saturday, 6.34am local time
Place: On the veranda of the house
         in the jungle. The biplane is now
         visible in the distance

In the glow of the rising sun, golden objects
glint and sparkle on a wicker chair. The
bright yellow water pistol is filled with
mosquito repellent. The notebook is full of
blank pages. Mysterious messages written
in invisible ink, perhaps? There's an object
here that was last seen in the hands of
someone very dangerous . . . It's time to
leave in a hurry.

Which object means danger, and why?

BACK TO THE BEGINNING

Time: Sunday, 9.54am
Place: Messiest desk, 120th Floor, Head Office
Diabolical Dyes & Inky Inks Incorporated

Back on familiar territory after a wasted journey and a good night's sleep. Is Professor Potts still in hiding as the coded message suggested? Not allowed to contact the *Potts Foundation*. Perhaps *Diabolical Dyes & Inky Inks Incorporated* holds some more clues. Hence a second visit. Looking in the mirror, the messiest desk looks different – and not just because it's a mirror image.

What items are missing?

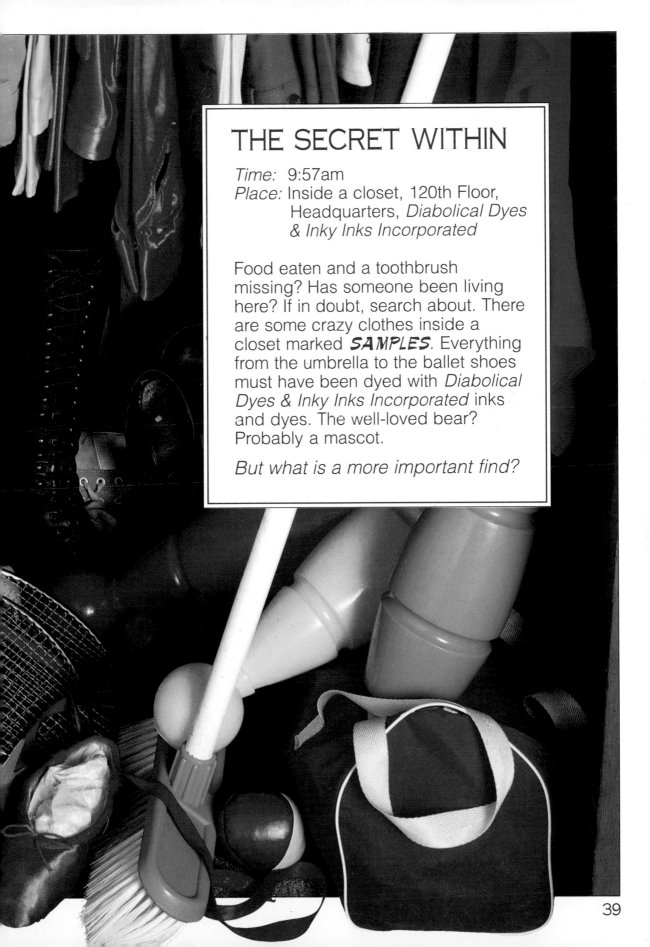

THE SECRET WITHIN

Time: 9:57am
Place: Inside a closet, 120th Floor,
        Headquarters, *Diabolical Dyes*
        & Inky Inks Incorporated

Food eaten and a toothbrush missing? Has someone been living here? If in doubt, search about. There are some crazy clothes inside a closet marked **SAMPLES**. Everything from the umbrella to the ballet shoes must have been dyed with *Diabolical Dyes & Inky Inks Incorporated* inks and dyes. The well-loved bear? Probably a mascot.

But what is a more important find?

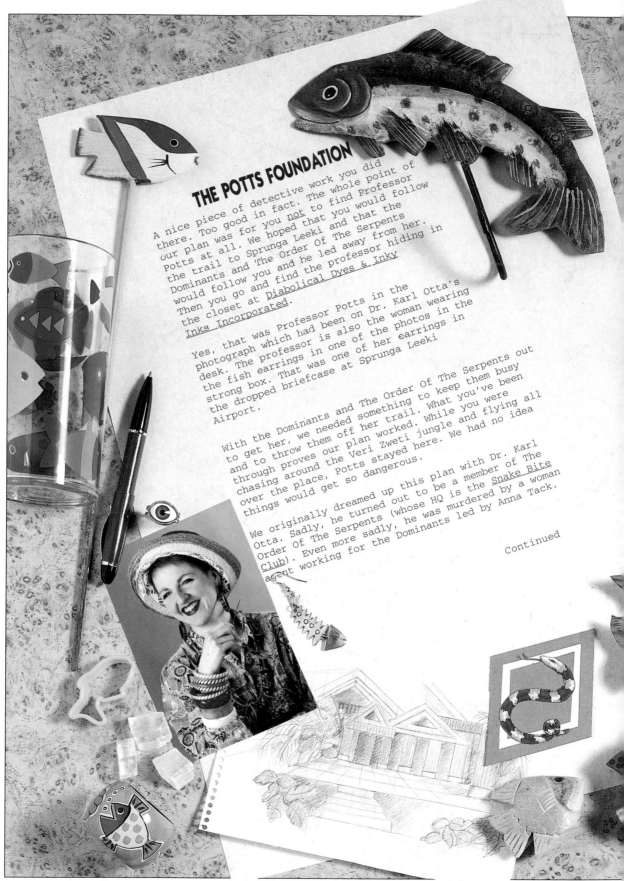

THE POTTS FOUNDATION

A nice piece of detective work you did there. Too good in fact. The whole point of our plan was for you <u>not</u> to find Professor Potts at all. We hoped that you would follow the trail to Sprunga Leeki and that the Dominants and The Order Of The Serpents would follow you and he led away from her. Then you go and find the professor hiding in the closet at <u>Diabolical Dyes & Inky Inks Incorporated.</u>

Yes, that was Professor Potts in the photograph which had been on Dr. Karl Otta's desk. The professor is also the woman wearing the fish earrings in one of the photos in the strong box. That was one of her earrings in the dropped briefcase at Sprunga Leeki Airport.

With the Dominants and The Order Of The Serpents out to get her, we needed something to keep them busy and to throw them off her trail. What you've been through proves our plan worked. While you were chasing around the Veri Zweti jungle and flying all over the place, Potts stayed here. We had no idea things would get so dangerous.

We originally dreamed up this plan with Dr. Karl Otta. Sadly, he turned out to be a member of The Order Of The Serpents (whose HQ is the <u>Snake Bite Club</u>). Even more sadly, he was murdered by a woman agent working for the Dominants led by Anna Tack.

Continued

*Must remember to order
some more Potts
Foundation letterheaded
paper*

The man who dropped his case was a member of
the T.O.O.T.S. keeping an eye on you in the
hope of finding the professor. (He must have
found one of her fish earrings when on the
trail.)

Now that her research has been published,
Professor Potts is free to live a normal
again. Congratulations on all your hard wo

Next week, the professor flies to Mount Thunder
in search of the Lost Lettuce of Phoenix Rock.
Until then, she plans to do some weeding in the
garden.

Maxwell Thorne

Maxwell Thorne
Vice-President

*P.S. Sorry about the fake money
we paid you for expenses. It came
from Dr. Karl Otta before we
realized that he was mixed up
with the gangs.*

41

HELPFUL HINTS

PAGES 2 & 3
Try matching the large bugs to the smaller ones.

PAGES 4 & 5
Dates aren't just a sort of fruit.

PAGES 6 & 7
Try removing the capital letters.

PAGES 8 & 9
Things that tell the time hold the vital clues.

PAGES 10 & 11
Look back at Dr. Karl Otta – or what we can see of him.

PAGES 12 & 13
There are more than just notices on the noticeboard.

PAGES 14 & 15
Where else have you seen similar money?

PAGES 16 & 17
Look back to pages 8 & 9.

PAGES 18 & 19
Look at the first letter of each word in the coded clue. This should help you to use the map!

PAGES 20 & 21
Can you see anything familiar? Look back to pages 8 & 9.

PAGES 22 & 23
"Fishy in more ways than one" is important here. The object was last seen in a photograph of someone.

PAGES 24 & 25
You've only seen a picture of it before now.

PAGES 26 & 27
Look back to Professor Potts's journal on pages 18 &19.

PAGES 28 & 29
A mirror might help you.

PAGES 30 & 31
It will help if you look back to what Potts said on page 19 about animals in the Veri Zweti jungle.

PAGES 32 & 33
Study the symbols carefully.

PAGES 34 & 35
You'll need a clue from the photos in the safety deposit box on pages 6 & 7 and some information from Potts's journal on pages 18 & 19.

PAGES 36 & 37
The answers are a mouthful.

PAGES 38 & 39
Someone has put her foot in it.

ANSWERS

PAGES 2 & 3

The card covered in small bugs and a meaningless message is, in fact, the key to the real message. Match the bugs on the numbered cards against the bugs on the key card. Write down the words to the right of the matching bugs, and then read them in the order of the numbered cards 1 to 8. The message reads:
Take the key from under the box of dates on the messiest desk in the building.

PAGES 4 & 5

The word *dates* in the message is not referring to dates as in fruit. It is referring to dates as in the day and the month. The key is under the box-shaped calendar.

PAGES 6 & 7

The capital letters spell out the name *PROFESSOR POTTS* over and over again. Remove them and you will be left with a message. Decoded and with punctuation added it reads:
Here is a car key belonging to the one person photographed without an animal. Visit the person at once.

PAGES 8 & 9

The clock on the desk reads the correct time (3:27). Dr. Karl Otta's broken watch, however, reads 1:19. It is likely that the doctor's watch was broken when he was attacked. This means that he could have been attacked just over two hours ago.

PAGES 10 & 11

The snake symbol on the green book of matches is similar to the tiny snake tattoo on Dr. Karl Otta's hand on pages 9 & 10.

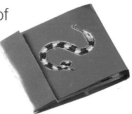

PAGES 12 & 13

Look at the notice that reads:
ALL HATS AND COATS TO BE CHECKED IN ON ARRIVAL. DON'T LOSE YOUR TICKET. NO TICKET, NO COAT. Next to it is a pink ticket that is similar to the pink ticket (Number 141) from the safety deposit box.

PAGES 14 & 15

All serial numbers on banknotes and bills are different. The number on this Sprunga Leeki dollar bill, however, matches the number on the top bill in the envelope marked **EXPENSES** on pages 6 & 7. This means that either some, or all, of this money is fake. Worthless.

PAGES 16 & 17

The framed photo of the woman is missing. In its place is an empty frame and a lipstick that wasn't there before.

PAGES 18 & 19

The first letter from each word under the journal entry:
"My whereabouts"
spells (with the correct spacing)
SQUARE A THREE. Square A3 in the map is on the middle of a jungle area. This was Potts's last location.

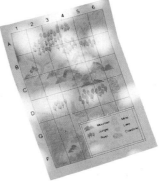

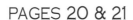

PAGES 20 & 21

Even though it is showing a different time, that is definitely Dr. Karl Otta's broken watch in the top left-hand corner of the case. The last time you saw it, it was on the dead man's wrist.

PAGES 22 & 23

There is a silver fish earring in the briefcase. It matches those worn by a woman in one of the torn-up photographs in the vault of the Third National Bank on pages 6 & 7.

PAGES 24 & 25

The spotted creature appears with the woman in a photograph. It's the one on Dr. Karl Otta's desk at his *Plant Import Export Company* on pages 8 & 9.

PAGES 26 & 27

Among the patterns drawn on the rock is the symbol and an arrow. The same symbol appears on pages 18 & 19. It is next to a note saying "My *secret sign*", in the professor's journal. The message on the rock, therefore, must be simply to follow the arrow.

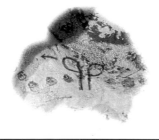

PAGES 28 & 29

The message is in mirror writing. Simply turn the book upside down and hold it in front of a mirror to read it. There's some very important information in this message, so read it carefully.

My life is in great danger now that I have found the special plant. It only grows inside the ruins of this great temple and is of interest to two powerful organizations. One, The Order of The Serpent, has kept this location and the plant's amazing powers a secret for a thousand years. Each member has a special snake tattoo.

The other organization has evil aims. Called the Dominants, its members plan to use some of the special plant's powers as a mind control drug. They want to turn the population into mindless slaves. They each wear the ring of the Evil Eye.

Both groups want to stop my work. I'll only be safe when the report on my discoveries here are published. It includes the formula to an antidote to the mind control drug. Once that is done, it will be too late for them to try to silence me. Until then, I shall go into hiding. So, whoever is reading this, please understand that I don't want to be found. Go home.

POTTS

PAGES 30 & 31

In Friday's entry in the journal on pages 18 & 19, Professor Potts describes the deekay lizard as "the only poisonous creature in the whole country...". This would suggest that the snake here is harmless ... Then again, it might have been flown in from abroad!

PAGES 32 & 33

The eye symbol on the large water bottle matches an eye symbol on a piece of crumpled paper. The paper is on pages 20 & 21 – on a woman's briefcase on-board *Flight 01424* to Sprunga Leeki.

The woman on the plane is wearing an eye ring. In Potts's message left in the ruins of the temple on pages 28 & 29, you are told that members of the Dominants wear "*the ring of the Evil Eye*". This means that the woman must be a member of the dangerous Dominants gang – and connects this house in the jungle to the gang. Beware!

PAGES 34 & 35

You have seen this giant pocket watch somewhere before. It appeared in a photograph from the safety deposit box on pages 6 & 7. It was held by a woman wearing an eye patch. In the journal on pages 18 & 19, Potts has written that the "*evil Anna Tack, the woman with the eye patch, is the leader of the ruthless Ds. She is a very dangerous woman.*"

From the information on 28 & 29, it is obvious that by writing Ds, the professor means the Dominants. The giant pocket watch must belong to Anna Tack herself.

PAGES 36 & 37

Cherries and cakes have been eaten, and the toothbrush is missing from the pen holder by the telephone. Perhaps the person who ate the food then brushed his, or her, teeth?

PAGES 38 & 39

Look closely and you'll see that there are trouser legs coming out of the top of those boots. Someone is hiding in the *SAMPLES* closet!

DID YOU KNOW?

There is at least one fish on every double page – from fish-shaped keyrings to a fish bookmark.

On pages 40 & 41, you'll find most of the fish that appear elsewhere in the book. But not all. Some fish are missing and some are new. See if you can tell which are which.

DID YOU SPOT?

Dr. Karl Otta wasn't the only one with a snake tattoo. A man in one of the safety deposit box photographs, on pages 6 & 7, had one on his cheek as well.

There were edible hats in the box on pages 30 & 31. Professor Potts mentioned them in the journal on pages 18 & 19.

On pages 4 & 5, the clock on the messiest desk at the headquarters of *Diabolical Dyes & Inky Inks Incorporated* had stopped. On pages 36 & 37, however, it is showing a different time of day . . . but still the wrong one.

The car rental company advertised on the Snake Bite Club noticeboard on pages 12 & 13 is called TOOTS Car Rental. Did you realize that TOOTS stood for The Order Of The Serpent?

In the photograph on pages 40 & 41, Professor Potts was wearing some of the bracelets from the trunk on pages 24 & 25.

The crystals in the tin on pages 26 & 27, appeared next to the photograph of Potts on pages 40 & 41. They are made from the special plant that caused all the trouble.

The tiny snakes on pages 30 & 31 might not be plastic after all. One of them appears to be eating some fruit.

First published in 1995 by Usborne Publishing Limited, Usborne House, 83-85 Saffron Hill, London EC1N 8RT, England.
© Copyright 1995 Usborne Publishing Ltd.
The name Usborne and the device ⊕ are Trade marks of Usborne Publishing Ltd. All rights reserved.
Printed in Spain   U.E. First published in America August 1995